Splish, Splash, Flappy Ducks

by Ann Tobias

illustrations by
Dubravka Kolanovic

The rain poured down.
"It's a beautiful day,"
said Mama Duck,
"a perfect day for little
ducklings to play outside."

"I don't like the rain," said Fluffy Duck.
"It makes my fuzzy feathers flat."
"I don't like the rain," said Flappy Duck.
"It makes me sneeze. ACHOO!"

"I don't like the rain," said Fancy Duck.
"My feet get muddy."

"Ducks like rain," said Mama Duck,
and she opened the door for the ducklings.

"I wish we could go to the movies," said Fluffy Duck. "It's warm and dry there."

"I wish we could go to the library," said Flappy Duck. "It's warm and dry there too. *ACHOO!*"

"I wish we could go home and play with our toys," said Fancy Duck. "But Mama doesn't like muddy footprints."

"This rain is making my sandwich soggy," said Fluffy Duck.

"It is making my lemonade watery," said Flappy Duck. "*ACHOO!*"

"It is making my cookie fall apart," said Fancy Duck.

Out came the sun, and the ducklings spent
the whole afternoon jumping rope, running races,
and rowing in
the pond.

"My feathers are fuzzy again," said Fluffy.

"I have stopped sneezing," said Flappy.

"But we are still making
muddy footprints,"
said Fancy.

At the end of the day the ducklings happily waddled home, splashing through so many puddles that their feet were washed clean.